MY SIDE OF THE CAR

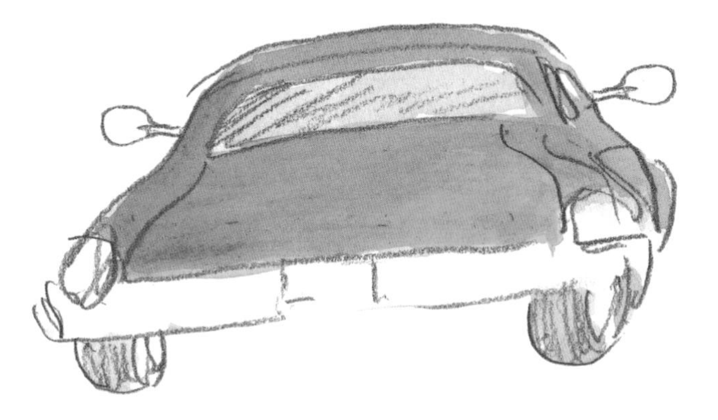

Kate Feiffer

illustrated by Jules Feiffer

CANDLEWICK PRESS

My dad and I are going to the zoo.

We’ve tried to go to the zoo before. But we never get there.
Something always happens.

One day when we were supposed to go to the zoo,
my mom tripped over a toy fire engine.

So we went to the hospital instead of the zoo.

Another day when we were supposed to go to the zoo,
my dog, Pasha, got lost.

So we spent the day looking for him instead of going to the zoo.

Another day when we were supposed to go to the zoo, my grandparents showed up for a surprise visit. And they don't like the zoo.

So we went to the museum instead of the zoo.

Today we're finally going to the zoo. Nothing can stop us.
Not a broken foot. Or a lost dog . . . or a surprise visit.

Not even an escaped tiger.

Because if we don't go to the zoo today,
I don't think we will ever get there.

The monkeys and giraffes and elephants and
polar bears have waited a long time to see us.

We're finally on our way. We're having the best time ever.

Until my dad says to me, "Sadie, it's raining."

I look out my window and say to him, “No, it’s not.”

Then he says it again: “Sadie, it’s raining. We can’t go to the zoo.”

So I look out my window again and say,
“It’s not raining on my side of the car.”

My dad keeps driving. After a few minutes, he says, "Sadie, is it raining on your side of the car yet?"

I look out my window, and the sun is shining on my side of the car. People are putting on their sunglasses and heading to zoos all over the world on my side of the car.

My dad keeps driving.

After he drives a little longer, he says, “Sadie, it’s pouring on my side of the car. I think by now it must be at least drizzling on your side of the car.”

So I look out my window again.
One drop has fallen on my side of the car.

It might not even be a whole drop. It looks more like half a drop.

The huge field of sunflowers we're driving by won't even notice half a drop.

So I tell him, "It's not raining on my side of the car.
People on my side of the car are watering their lawns."

After we pass two stop signs and drive up a big hill, my dad says, “Sadie, what about now? It’s raining so hard on my side of the car that the windshield wipers are exhausted.

Is it even sprinkling on your side of the car yet?”

The rain from his side of the car made a puddle that splashed my side of the car, so I can't see all the people . . .

who I know are there, walking their dogs or
riding their bikes or eating ice cream.

I tell him, “No, it’s still not raining on my side of the car.”

He keeps driving.

The roads on his side of the car look more like rivers than roads.

So we decide to look for roads on my side of the car
because the zoo is on my side of the car.

After an extra long trip, we finally get to the zoo.

“We’re here,” says my dad.

I get out and walk over to his side of the car.
"What do you think?" he asks.

“I think that it’s raining really hard on your side of the car, and I don’t want you to get wet,” I say. “We should come back to the zoo another day.”

“Okay,” says my dad. “So do I.”

After a big turn and a hill and some boring, just plain roads, my dad says,

“Sadie, I was wondering if it’s raining on your side of the car, because it stopped raining on my side of the car.”

Off we go. We're going to the zoo.

At last!

Father and daughter discuss the real-life event that inspired *My Side of the Car:*

Jules: We were on Martha's Vineyard. You must have been eight or nine or ten, whatever it was. You were sitting in the backseat of the car. We had started off to go to Felix Neck Wildlife Sanctuary, which you loved to go to. As we got about a mile or so away from the house, it began to rain, and I said, "Uh-oh, Katie, I don't think we can go because it's raining." You looked out your window and said, "It's not raining on my side of the car."

Kate: Because it wasn't.

Jules: Of course it was raining.

Kate: It was not raining.

Jules: Of course it was raining. You just had decided you were going to Felix Neck no matter what, even when it began to pour.

Kate: It wasn't raining on my side of the car.

Jules: It was pouring on my side of the car. And it was nice and sunny on your side of the car? (Sigh.) Anyhow, there you were, and there I was, being your chauffeur and trying to take care of my daughter and not get her soaked, and you weren't having any part of it.

Kate: Because it wasn't raining on my side of the car.

Jules: Well, there we go. And that is that.

For Sarah Hill
K. F.

For Katie, then and now
J. F.

First edition 2011

Library of Congress Cataloging-in-Publication Data is available.
Library of Congress Card Number pending
ISBN 978-0-7636-4405-5

11 12 13 14 15 16 17 SCP 10 9 8 7 6 5 4 3 2 1

Printed in Humen, Dongguan, China

This book was typeset in Clichee.
The illustrations were done in watercolor and pencil.

Candlewick Press
99 Dover Street
Somerville, Massachusetts 02144

visit us at www.candlewick.com